Contents

Chapter 1

Promises, Promises

I have a little brother. His name is Tim. He is four-and-a-half years old and he gets into trouble all the time.

After he gets into trouble, Tim always says, "I'll be good now."

Five minutes later, he does something even worse.

Like when he pulled the stuffing out of
my teddy bear. He buried it in the back
garden. He told Mum that he thought he
had killed it.

"Tim's only a little boy, Mandy," Mum
says. "He'll grow out of it."

I don't think that will ever happen.

Today Tim was worse than ever. It was the day our parents came to school to see our classroom.

My teacher's name is Miss Monk. "We're sure to have a lovely time," she said.

I had been looking forward to it. That
was until Mum told me that Tim would be
coming too.

"Why can't he stay at Nana's house?" I
asked. "Miss Monk didn't invite him."

"Don't worry, Mandy. I'm going to be
good this time," Tim promised.

Chapter 2

Tim's Monkey

The parents were due at 10 o'clock. Mum and Tim were the first to arrive.

As Tim ran through the door, he said, "Hello, Miss Monkey."

"My name is Miss Monk," my teacher told him.

Some of the children giggled. They stopped when they saw the look on Miss Monk's face.

"Hello everybody!" Tim yelled to the class. "I'm Mandy's brother."

My teacher smiled at Mum. She didn't smile at Tim. Miss Monk didn't like being called a monkey.

While Mum and Miss Monk talked about school, Tim hopped around the room. Next thing I knew he was standing on Miss Monk's chair. Tim held his hands under his chin. Then he began to jump up and down.

"I'm a kangaroo," he said as he jumped higher and higher. "I can jump as high as the sky."

"Get down before you fall," Miss Monk growled.

"I don't think Miss Monkey likes me," Tim said. Mum grabbed his arm and dragged him to the back of the room.

Chapter 3

Cuckoo Calls

Soon the room was full of parents. The class sat up and looked at Miss Monk — just like she'd told us to do.

"Let's say a big welcome to our mums and dads," said Miss Monk.

"Welcome to our classroom," we all said.
"We hope you like our work."

"The children would like to sing you some songs," Miss Monk said as she sat at the piano.

The first song was called 'The Cuckoo Song'. It sounded good ... at first!

A horrible noise was coming from the back of the room. It was Tim singing as loudly as he could. He was making up the words and yelling cuckoo all the time.

Mum put her hand over his mouth. She
pulled it off after Tim bit her on the
finger. Tim was in trouble again.

"I was only trying to help," he sobbed.

Our songs ended. Tim stopped crying. He crawled under some desks and made a dash for the piano.

"We will now sing 'Baa Baa Black Sheep'," he said as he thumped the keys with his fists.

I knew what I'd like to thump and it wasn't the piano.

Miss Monk gave Tim some blocks. She told him to sit in the corner and play with them.

"That should keep him quiet for awhile," I thought.

I was wrong.

Chapter 4

See You Next Year

Tim made a train. That was fine. He made a truck. That was good too. Then he threw the blocks in the air. Tim said they were planes — planes flying through the sky.

But the planes fell down on people's heads!

"Do *try* to behave," Mum told Tim. Her face was red. She was really annoyed.

"I'm going to learn to read now," Tim said as he ran to the bookshelf.

"I have a better idea," Miss Monk said as she rushed to save our new books.

"Why don't you learn to draw instead? Go and sit next to Mandy while I get you some paper."

Tim didn't want to learn to draw. He wanted to clean the board. That would be more fun.

Before anyone could stop him, Tim rubbed out most of Miss Monk's work.

"I was only trying to help you," Tim told Miss Monk.

Miss Monk said something but I don't
think she was thanking him for his help.

Tim was quiet. He came and sat beside me.

"What are you eating?" I asked.

"A sandwich," he mumbled. He poked the
last bit into his mouth.

"Where did you get it?" I asked. I didn't
really want to know.

Tim pointed to Miss Monk's basket.

"That was her lunch," I groaned.

He held out an apple. "I got this for you, Mandy," Tim said with a smile.

I *knew* where the apple had come from. "You'll get me into trouble," I hissed. "Put it back."

Then the recess bell rang. It was time for the parents to leave. Miss Monk thanked them for coming.

"I start school next year. I'm going to ask if I can be in your class," Tim told Miss Monk.

Miss Monk didn't answer. I think she was wondering if she could move to another school.

Glossary

arrive
come

cuckoo
a bird with a 'cuckoo' call

growled
spoke in a low, angry voice

hissed
annoyed speech

promise
something that you will do

recess
morning break, little lunch

stuffing
the filling of a toy

thumped
hit very hard

Jan Weeks

Here are some of my favourite 'Why?' questions.

1. Why is a boxing ring square?

2. Why doesn't glue stick to the inside of the bottle?

3. Why is the time of day with the slowest traffic called 'rush hour'?

4. Why isn't there mouse-flavoured cat food?

5. Why don't we ever see the newspaper headline, 'Fortune Teller Wins Lotto'?

6. Why is it that rain drops and snow falls?

Janine Dawson